GOING BACK TO MOVE FORWARD

A Baby Boomer's Time Travel

A NOVELLA BY

JOHN SPONCIA

ISBN: 1500257001
ISBN-13: 9781500257002

Straight Ahead Book Company
Menomonee Falls, Wisconsin

Acknowledgements

Special acknowledgements to Mrs. Whitney Roth and her fifth grade class at Marcy Elementary School in Menomonee Falls, WI and to Mr. Ted Schmidt and his seventh grade class at Silver Lake Middle School in Oconomowoc, WI.

As a volunteer, I was privileged to read this story to both classes, never realizing it had interest and appeal to a young audience. The students were totally engaged and invested in the story, and it was partially at their urging that I publish *Going Back to Move Forward*.

I give many thanks to these two special teachers and their students, for allowing me to share my story in their classrooms, and for helping to provide me with the motivation to self-publish this novella.

Finally, the character of the late Father James P. McDonald was a driving force in the development of this story, and (not coincidentally) he played an influential part in my early Catholic upbringing. My memories of him as a passionate priest, who loved and related well to his parishioners, remain crystal clear some fifty years later. Thank you and rest in peace, Father Mac!

TABLE OF CONTENTS

PREFACE

Author of the controversial commentary on today's culture, *Voiceover...Sanity in the Age of Madness,* John Sponcia now creates a personal narrative about time travel with a message attached to it.

Going Back to Move Forward is the author's fictional tale rooted in his own childhood experience. John Sponcia has spent much of his adult life comparing current life in America to the 1960s, a bygone era that he recalls as idyllic. He has secretly longed to somehow return to that time period, if even for a short time to once again experience a lifestyle he so fondly remembers.

In this novella, he is thrust back to 1960, arriving in his childhood neighborhood in Brooklyn, New York at his current age of sixty-four, forced to confront challenges for which he is totally unprepared. Feeling trapped and personally isolated, he takes the reader with him on his journey, attempting to reconcile the past with the present as he navigates back in time.

CHAPTER I

WELCOME BACK

It's that somewhat dazed feeling you have when you have first awakened, confused and disoriented. That's the feeling I have, but I am not in my bed. I am standing at a busy intersection in an urban commercial area. I look around searching for familiarity, a store, a landmark, a person I might know. It is then I realize I am in a totally different time period. I know this because I am very familiar with this era, but how did I wind up back in the 1960s?

I gaze into a storefront window. It is a sporting goods store and I see myself in the reflection. I am neither a child nor a teenager. I am at my present sixty-something age. I am wearing a zip-up hoodie with a Cleveland Browns' helmet silk-screened across the front, jeans, sneakers, and a baseball cap. This is my 'retirement uniform' or a mild variation of what I wear almost every day of my 'current life.'

I see a display of baseball bats selling for $2.99 with names like Yogi Berra, Duke Snider, and Willie Mays. Baseball gloves are "starting at $4.99" – there's a Whitey Ford Rawlings reminiscent of my own glove of fifty years ago. Wrangler brand "7-11" jeans are $2.99. How in the world did I end up back here again?

I walk along the crowded sidewalk of this somewhat familiar avenue and I see what looks like an old candy store. The fascia above the windows reads "Luncheonette – Fountain – Sodas" and emblazoned on this dark green background is a huge red Coca-Cola logo. I approach the glass door which reads "air-conditioned, it's cool inside." Smiling, but still puzzled and bewildered, I enter. Stacks of newspapers on a rack on the left and an impressive candy/gum display greets me while a middle-aged man with a cigarette hanging from his mouth feverishly works the cash register quickly processing customers as they eagerly pay for their purchases.

Further down there is a long counter with stools that is half-filled with patrons eating or awaiting the arrival of their order. I grab a seat and I am captivated by the memories evoked, but again I wonder how this is possible?

The counter clerk approaches me and I instinctive say "I'll have a large coke." Without so much as a nod of acknowledgement, he robotically reaches for a Coke glass (tapered at the bottom and flared at the top) from a freshly washed inventory of glasses that are sitting atop a white towel in a half-dried state. He positions the glass below a manual dispenser of dark brown syrup, delivers about two inches into the bottom so as to reach a measuring line that is marked around the circumference of the glass. He then fills the remainder with seltzer water emanating from a huge Coca-Cola display piece. He completes the order by stirring the solution with a long spoon. "Ten cents" he announces, expecting my payment as he sets the glass and a paper straw in front of me. I tender a quarter and he quickly returns fifteen cents back on the counter. I see a Buffalo nickel and a Mercury dime and I grin, thinking the 1984 GW quarter I gave him must not have appeared that different from those he has collected.

I am surrounded by people smoking as they eat and drink, so I swallow quickly and vacate my seat. Before exiting I reach for a newspaper and look at the date – it reads October 14, 1960 and the headline screams out "Yanks Lose Series on Mazeroski Home Run in Ninth!" I have now discovered the exact place in time into which I have landed!

I continue walking, but I now turn onto a residential street. As I wait for traffic to stop at the red light, I immediately notice the traffic light is mounted on a pedestal and stands on the sidewalk corner, as opposed to hanging above the center of the intersection. *"Yeah, I remember that"* I think to myself. A 1958 Chevy Impala streaks by and I admire those six taillights that highlight the rear end, identifying it as an Impala rather that Chevrolet's lower priced Bel-Air and Biscayne models. I was a student of automobile designs in my youth – certain pieces of information stay in your brain. Tail fins abound as Fords, Buicks, and Cadillacs cruise by…I am reminded there were very few imported cars back then.

The Chevron gas station across the street advertises gas at 25.9 cents a gallon and I see attendants pumping gas and rapidly washing windshields …Again a smile forms on my mouth.

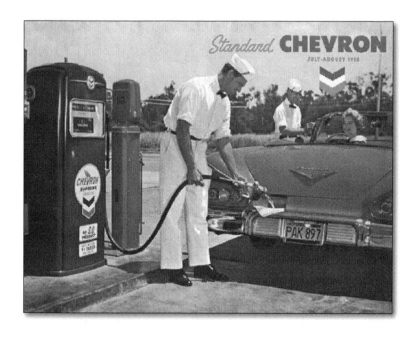

Young girls are playing on the sidewalk, which is covered with chalk designs of contiguous squares in an uneven arrangement. I think the game is hopscotch as I watch each girl hop through, alternating either on one leg or both to match the appropriate squares. Other children are mastering hula hoops, while even younger kids blow bubbles and watch them magically dissolve in mid-air. Seeing so many children outdoors, unsupervised, having fun without some mechanical device is alone an anomaly...But not for the time and place I am now re-immersed in!

I notice a delivery truck similar to a UPS truck, but this one is delivering baked goods. The driver parks his truck and exits carrying a large basket with a handle attached, overflowing with breads, cupcakes, muffins, and pies. He gives me a friendly nod, then rings a doorbell and is welcomed by the lady of the house and quickly invited in. He continues his route, walking from house to house selling his fresh baked goods. It was a trusting world in 1960!

As I continue walking through this residential area I cannot escape the plethora of political signage in the postage stamp-sized front yards, most of them imploring a vote for John F. Kennedy. I quickly realize the presidential election is less than a month away. It occurs to me that I am the only person certain of the outcome. I also know what will happen in three short years.

Have I been cursed? Have I been transported to "The Twilight Zone'? Where is Rod Serling hiding while smoking that ever-present cigarette? How can I fit into a world that's fifty years behind me...and how do I even begin to try to rejoin such an anachronistic environment? I have $35 in my pocket and a stack of credit cards that haven't yet been issued, and will be instantly rejected (assuming a store would even sell on credit). To complicate matters even further, I now realize precisely **where** I am...I have come full circle, back to the Flatbush section of Brooklyn, New York, my birthplace!

The afternoon sun has begun its descent, and the hint of a cool, autumn night fast-approaching, gets my attention. I need a place to stay tonight, and I haven't a clue what to do about it. My mind races for a solution and only one plausible alternative comes to mind. I will call my childhood home, and depending on who answers, I'll take it from there. My brain rewinds 52 years and the phone number rolls off my tongue...GEdney-4-0194. I enter a phone booth in a Rexall drug store. It reeks of stale cigarette smoke. I deposit my Mercury dime and methodically dial the number on the antiquated rotary dial system. As I wait for the number to process I stare up at a small, corner-mounted rubber fan...And I wonder, who will answer, and what will I say?

CHAPTER 2
BACK TO CHURCH

I listen intently as the telephone rings repetitively, continuing in an unending test of my patience. No voicemail in this lifetime, not even a 1970's answering machine that bellows your message throughout the house for all to hear. Fifteen rings is quite enough so I hang up the receiver and magically, I hear my dime land in the coin slot for me to recover…Ma Bell showing some integrity.

I ponder my next move – should I stake out my old home and simply show up at the front door and introduce myself…as whom? A long lost relative, an uncle researching his family tree? The truth isn't even a consideration. The men in blue from the 63rd Precinct would be summoned and I'd be hauled off to Bellevue Hospital for a psychiatric examination! I need a quiet place to think this through, to plan a strategy enabling me to readjust to this new life inside an old life. Exactly how does one navigate through this muddy mess?

I exit Rexall, first glancing at the analog wall clock over the door and it reads 4:35. I walk east on Glenwood Road leading in the direction of my old home, mulling over this conundrum as I walk. I approach Vanderveer

Park Methodist Church, which housed the first indoor basketball court I ever played on. We jokingly referred to it as the PYO, a play on words from CYO (Catholic Youth Organization). The glass-encased billboard proudly announces Sunday morning church service times.

As I pass the front steps I am delivered a lightning bolt from above...I'll continue walking six more blocks and enter the Catholic church of my youth, St. Vincent Ferrer! I am certain the doors will be open at this hour for anyone wishing to pray, light a candle for a deceased relative, or just sit in a pew and think in solitude. I hasten my gait as

I am anxious to see the Church, and maybe even some familiar faces from decades ago.

It is the same impressive four-story brick building, with the first two levels making up the church itself and the top two devoted to sixteen separate classrooms, accommodating grades one through eight of two classes each. I open the fortress-like front door and notice the small bulletin board on the wall. I approach, almost in trepidation, as I see this week's altar boy mass schedule, which is posted each Saturday by Father McDonald. This is a list you don't want your name at the top of, but there it is…'Kelly/Sponcia' @ 6:30 AM Monday thru Friday. Tim

Kelly and I seemed to draw an inordinate amount of early masses back in the day.

I walk up two sets of six marble steps and enter through the second set of doors, instinctively removing my baseball cap, and I sit down in the last pew. I gaze curiously recollecting the many hours I spent on these hard wooden benches, alternating in the repetitive sit-stand-kneel process of a typical mass. A middle-aged woman kneeling at the altar rail is saying a prayer after lighting a votive candle, the only other visitor on this late afternoon. She finishes and begins the long walk down the center aisle. As she draws closer to me I cannot believe my eyes…It is Mrs. Shaw, my next-door neighbor! Her eyes are cast down in reverence, but it is indeed her! I reject my impulse to stop her and say hello. After all, who am I to her but an inappropriately dressed, sixtyish stranger who is seeking refuge in the Church.

My frustration with my plight intensifies as I see more clearly the innate difficulty this journey back has posed for me. I am a man without a purpose, without a friend, and most importantly, without a plan for my new future.

As Mrs. Shaw exits, I hear a friendly exchange of greetings in the lobby and the door pops open and a man dressed in black emerges. I glance and immediately recognize Father James P. McDonald, the charismatic priest referenced earlier.

Our eyes meet, and he then approaches me with a smile and says "Good afternoon sir, do you need help with anything?" I probably resembled a borderline homeless man, since most people of that era would never enter a church dressed as I was (Maybe Mrs. Shaw busted me as an outsider seeking refuge in the arms of the Church).

"Thank you father, I'm fine – just seeking some solitude in God's house. I am visiting some relatives. Actually it's a surprise visit, but I have been the one surprised as I now realize they must be out of town, since their house is dark and no one answered the phone." *I immediately wonder if there was some greater punishment in hell for those lying to a priest. Perhaps some 'super-furnace' in a distant subterranean wing…Why did I come up with this lame story?*

The priest took a seat next to me and in an affable manner he began to engage in a conversation: "A great idea, but it's too bad it didn't work out. My name is Father McDonald," and he extended his hand in a vice-like grip instantly identifying him as an alpha-male type.

"Pleasure to meet you Father, I'm John Spinella", blurting out my second lie in the last thirty seconds. "I am a Catholic but my relatives who live in this neighborhood are not Catholic. My niece married a Protestant and became a Lutheran. Didn't go over very well with some of the family but we have remained close. I guess I have a more tolerant view of religious preference." *('Oh what a tangled web we weave,' I thought).*

"We are all God's children, John. It's good that you have remained close to your niece's family. What's your plan until they show up?"

"Well, I really haven't thought it through…Just sitting here in church to think about it. I guess for the moment, find a place to get some dinner" I made a mental note that this response was the first truthful one I uttered. I was a bit incredulous at the level of engagement our conversation was progressing, and I was truly stunned by what he said next.

"Do you like Italian food? What am I thinking, of course you do! There's a great restaurant close by – would you like to join me for pizza and beer?"

I immediately thought of *Michael's* an informal restaurant near the church. It was one with a connecting barroom, where I frequently bought pizza for carry-out back in my youth. I was totally taken aback by such a friendly gesture – Father Mac always seemed like a pizza and beer kind of guy, but as a kid I looked at him as an authority figure to be feared and respected. Now, as a person at least twenty years his senior, I was being invited to dinner?

"Yes, thank you Father. That sounds wonderful"

"Excellent! We'll take my car. It's parked by the Rectory a block away. You finish praying and I'll pick you up in front of the church in fifteen minutes."

He left quickly and I was alone again, wondering where all this would lead and how I would answer what I assumed would be a multitude of questions. And how many more lies could I tell to a priest I held in the highest esteem without caving? I prayed for direction and left the building. Darkness had completely descended over Brooklyn and the crisp autumn air swept over my face. A black Ford Galaxie approached with Father Mac at the wheel motioning me to get in. I smiled and thought… *Just let this play out. How bad of an outcome could it be?*

CHAPTER 3
HANGIN' OUT WITH FATHER MAC

As I enter the car I instinctively reach for the seatbelt/shoulder harness that I am so accustomed to using, but I am jolted back to my new reality. Not even the lap belt had been mandated as safety equipment in 1960. I suddenly felt a tad vulnerable as Father Mac wheeled his big sled westbound onto Glenwood Road.

The soulful sound of Sam Cooke's voice singing *Chain Gang* filled the passenger compartment, followed by WMCA's disc jockey 'Dandy Dan Daniel' counting down the week's Top Ten Hits! *Father Mac listening to rock 'n roll... Who knew?*

The priest leaned toward the dashboard and turned down the volume. *Here it comes – get set for the inquisition.* "You're gonna like this place, John, it's just around the corner. We could have walked but they're saying it may rain tonight so it's best we drive. I've known Michael the owner for years. When I need a break from 'rectory food' this is the place I go. Sometimes I'll even walk here for a nightcap at the bar."

This is getting stranger by the moment...Father Mac crushing boilermakers at *Michael's Restaurant and Bar* at midnight. Actually, not that much of a stretch to imagine! "I'm looking forward to it Father, I'm pretty hungry."

In less than two minutes we are there. The priest maneuvers his full-size sedan (ALL were full-size back then) into a tight parking space and we enter the restaurant.

Memories come flooding back to me. The right entrance door leads to the bar and the left door opens to the dining room. Tables on the left side and a row of booths line the wall on the right side of the room. I couldn't make this comparison in my first go-around in 1960, but it actually resembles the Italian restaurant in *The*

Godfather where Michael Corleone put a bullet in Captain McCluskey's forehead.

We seat ourselves in a booth and a waitress appears and greets Father Mac like an old friend. "Who's your buddy, Father?"

"Fran, this is John, a friend of mine…Start us off with a couple of cold ones."

Glancing at me she reels off the beer list: "We have Schaefer, Miller, Rheingold, and Piels on tap, Budweiser and Pabst in a bottle if you like." Tempted as I was to request a Miller Lite (which hadn't yet been invented), I opted for a glass of Piels, a brand whose advertising pitchmen were Bert and Harry Piels, two brothers who advertised their beer as "glorious" back in the day.

"And Fran, can you get a pizza started for us right away. I've been bragging about your pizza to John and we are both more than ready for it?"

"Will do, Father, and a Schaefer in a mug for you, comin' right up." She smiled while tucking her pad in the apron pocket on her way to the kitchen.

Within two minutes our beers landed on the table and the priest raised his glass in a toast: "Here's to new friends, John. God places people on a path with a purpose in mind." Our glasses met and as I looked into his steely blue eyes I felt like he knew more about me than I wanted him to. After the first gulp he cleared his throat and gave me a pensive look, then a pause as he might do when he was about to make an important point from the pulpit in a Sunday sermon. "John, I know your story is bogus *(now there's word from the 60s I hadn't heard in decades but hearing that right out of the blue immediately made me uncomfortable)*, but I want you to be truthful and answer this one question...Have you committed a crime? Whatever it is, you can confide in me."

I paused with a sigh of relief. He was giving me a pass on full disclosure and I did not hesitate. "Father I'm very sorry I lied to you, but no, I haven't done anything wrong and I am not running from anyone. If I were, would I be here with you in a public place?"

I sensed from his expression that he believed me and I felt even better when he answered "I'll respect your privacy but at the same time, I'd like to help you any way I can. I have a feeling you are experiencing some huge internal struggle. Am I right, John?"

At that moment our pizza arrived enabling a temporary diversion off the topic. "Good idea to get here early Father," Fran said as she set the round aluminum pan between us. "Friday nights are always busy, thanks to the Catholics. Seems like it's either fish or pizza for dinner. Ya think that 'no meat on Friday' rule will ever change Father?"

"Not in our lifetimes, Fran...It's a small sacrifice to make." I smiled, knowing this Church law would be gone in the not too distant future. I thought of George Carlin's remark about all those Friday meat-eaters suffering in hell. Would they now be promoted to at least purgatory, he wondered?

"Great choice, Father," I mumbled after my first bite. "I had a feeling I'd like this place, it has a familiar feel to it."

"Glad you are comfortable John, but let me ask...Where are you spending the night and where are your things? I know one thing for sure...you're NOT from around here."

`I was in the middle of a bite and I used every available second to decide how I would answer this 'second' question. My response would dictate my new future. I swallowed and reached for my glass to buy a few more seconds. Meanwhile, Father James Patrick McDonald sat with his elbows on the table, with hands folded under his chin, anxiously awaiting my answer.

CHAPTER 4
SHOWDOWN

Father James P. McDonald was not a complicated man. To some teenage boys of the 1950s and 60s, he appeared to be the kind of priest who made the priesthood actually seem like it could be a fun job. He conducted his job as if he reported to no one but God Himself. He seemed to be quite independent, with his primary responsibilities centering on young people's activities. He supervised the Friday night church dances and other social events like roller skating bus trips. He was also instrumental in forming a Little League baseball team which competed with other parish teams in Brooklyn.

Father Mac had what some would describe as a 'personal flair' attached to everything he did. When he walked into a room, he owned it! His sermons were always passionate and sometimes very compelling. You felt like he was speaking directly to you as opposed to the entire congregation. This may be a bit of a leap but he was kind of JFK-ish, in a religious sense. One thing was indisputable...You didn't want to get on the wrong side of this guy.

With good looks and a dynamic personality, Father Mac was a 'no nonsense' kind of priest. His confessional booth consistently had the longest line every Saturday because there wasn't a sin you were afraid to confess to him. He was non-judgmental and your penance never varied…Five Hail Marys and you were good to go! In short he was a 'man's man' who was likeable, but also respected by all for his candor, work ethic, and genuine concern for all his parishioners.

And now I am in a showdown with someone whom I know will not back down until he uncovers the truth. He could have been a great detective if not a priest. His questions were direct and unyielding, and his approach was relentless.

"Father, you're right - I'm not from around here and I don't have any of my clothes or possessions with me." I thought for a moment and qualified my response a bit. "Actually I used to be from here so I am familiar with the area. More than that, I cannot tell you at this time. I really wish I could give you more information – please trust me – I'm not a bad person and you were correct when you said I am having some internal struggles."

Mercifully, Fran arrives with a second round of beers and removes the empty glasses. "You gentlemen need anything else?"

"We're doing fine Fran, everything's great as usual. Say hello to Michael for me. I know he took the night off. When you get a moment, bring me the check." The priest smiled at her as she nodded and picked up the empty pizza pan from the table.

I looked across the table to get a reaction to what amounted to a very awkward admission on my part. The priest was staring right back at me, and I think he was feeling my strife and began to back down a bit.

"Okay John, I'll give you the time and space you need to gain my trust. I meant what I said about helping you so I'm going to suggest a proposition. Since it's apparent you need a few staples to get you through at least the next few days, let's take a short ride after dinner. There's a department store named Korvette's not too far from here, and their clothes are reasonably priced We'll pick up a few items until your own gear arrives. There's a guest room in the rectory that visitors use on occasion…You can bunk there for a little while until you sort all this out." Then he stopped talking to measure my reaction.

I was dumbfounded! He must have sensed this and said "Don't worry about it John…It will all work itself out. Let's face it, it doesn't appear to me that you have a lot of friends here, or a lot of alternative choices available to you at this time. Have I got that right?" *(Spoken like a man who was holding all the cards)*

The good Father was right on both counts so I smiled and answered sheepishly, "You are too kind Father, thank you so much. You are literally a Godsend."

"As I said earlier John, God places all of us on a path. We need to trust in Him and just let everything else unfold," he responded with great sincerity.

We left after Father Mac picked up the check (4 beers and a pizza for under $10…Are you kidding me?)

I vividly recalled E. J. Korvette, a popular retailer of this bygone era similar to today's Target but with a greater emphasis on clothing. I was able to pick up some needed toiletries, underwear, and a few shirts for a total of $23, leaving me an Alexander Hamilton and two GWs in my billfold. I observed in amazement how slow and cumbersome the checkout process was as the salesclerk keyed in each amount and the cash register mechanically calculated all the items. This was akin to the Stone Age compared to the computerized scanners of the 21st century. So much was so different!

It is approaching nine o'clock as we pull into the driveway adjacent to the Rectory. It occurs to me that I had never been past the vestibule of this building that housed the revered priests of my childhood, and now it would be my temporary shelter. We walk through the back door entering a kitchen that was sparkling clean and dark except for a pull cord fluorescent tube light above the sink. A bowl of fruit sat in the center of the kitchen table. Dishes were drying in the rack. A white Sears Coldspot refrigerator with only one door and no sign of a dishwasher were further indications as to what decade I was now living in.

Father Mac leads the way through a hallway as we bypass a living room where I hear voices and laughter. The TV is loud enough to discern the iconic voice of Don

Dunphy broadcasting the *"Friday Night Fights,"* a legendary weekly sports event that captivated American men of that era. Boxing was actually a very popular sport, and this was Friday night 'must see TV'.

"Is that you, Jim?" A voice emanated from the room.

"Yeah Walt …It's me and I have someone with me." We backtracked into the living room and there were Fathers Murphy and Spengler, smoking cigarettes and dressed in everyday 'civilian' casual clothes. "John, I want you to meet Father Walter Murphy and Father Raymond Spengler."

As I extended my hand in greeting to Father Murphy, he set his Manhattan on a coaster and welcomed me with a big smile. His six foot frame wasn't quite as intimidating as I recall in bygone days when he towered over me by almost a foot…Now we were almost at eye level. Father Spengler was of much smaller stature and he was also amiable, just as I remember him. Of the two, Father 'Murph' was the one I remember having a distinct fondness for altar wine and it appeared tonight he was opting for the harder stuff.

"John's going to be our houseguest for a few days… he'll take the guestroom. When does Gately get back from his vacation, Ray?" He was referring to Father William Gately, the Pastor who, in his day was the most feared and least popular of all the priests in the parish. Serving as his altar boy was an adventure in anxiety, having to acquaint yourself with all of his individual idiosyncrasies and special requirements he demanded.

He made it clear he was the big Kahuna and this was **HIS** church. *I was glad to hear he was gone tonight.*

"Middle of next week, Jim," Spengler replied.

"Okay, great, John's had a long day so I'll get his room set up and join you in a few minutes. I wanna catch the feature fight."

"Welcome to Saint Vincent's, John, see you in the morning," both priests echo as we exit back into the hallway.

He escorts me to a very tidy bedroom, points out the location of the bathroom in the hall, and asks if I need anything else. "We have a cook and housekeeper who arrives every morning at 5 AM. You'll like Mildred, great cook and very efficient. She keeps all of us guys in line," he says with a smile. "I don't have a mass tomorrow but I'm always up by seven. I'll see you in the morning…Sleep as late as you want."

"I'm a morning person, Father so I'll be up when you are" I answer. "I can't thank you enough for all you are doing for me."

"Get a good night's sleep, John. You look like you need it." I shut the bedroom door and sit down on side of the bed. I gaze across the room at a framed reproduction of a painting of Jesus praying in the Garden of Gethsemane prior to his arrest and crucifixion.

A thousand images race through my mind as I come to the end of day one of this odyssey, a trip back in time fifty-two years. Tonight I would sleep in a bed in a building that was less than a hundred yards from my boyhood home. Do I dare walk down the street tomorrow and sneak a peek at my own life and family? Can all this be possible? It's so hard to even imagine. I lay back on the bed in total mental and physical exhaustion. My eyes close and darkness becomes my closest friend.

CHAPTER 5

SATURDAY MORNING

Exhaustion has a way of ruling your body. When there is no more gas in the tank, your body reacts in a predictable way...You sleep a lot. And so, if not for the unmistakable aroma of bacon frying in a pan and drifting into my bedroom sending a distinct message to my olfactory nerve, I may have slept until noon. I glance at the clock radio on the nightstand and it reads 6:30. I realize I slept for nine hours without awakening, unheard of in my 'normal' life. Furthermore, I slept in my clothes after collapsing on the bed. The bathroom is unoccupied so I take a quick shower. There is a supply of Gem disposable razor blades, a double-edged razor, and shaving cream on the counter so I lather up and by 6:45 I feel like a new man (*which I am beginning to believe I am*).

I slip on my jeans and one of the long sleeve shirts I bought at Korvette's and I am reasonably presentable for breakfast. Father Mac is seated at the kitchen table reading *The Daily News* as Mildred is supervising the bacon and eggs cooking on the stove. She is middle-aged and clad in a housedress with an apron to shield from the splatter created by what smells like a delicious, high caloric and fat gram-loaded breakfast. I remind myself these health-conscious thoughts are not on anyone's radar screen in 1960. 'If it tastes good, eat it', is the mantra of this era.

Father Mac makes introductions and I receive a warm welcome from Mildred followed by "How do you like your eggs, or would you rather have pancakes?"

"I like 'em scrambled, Mildred, and thanks for asking," I responded without hesitating.

"Coffee's in the percolator on the counter, John. Help yourself. Would you like an English Muffin or white toast?"

I eye the familiar package of Thomas English muffins (some things never change) and opt for the 'nooks and crannies' while pouring myself a mug of perked coffee, as it was referred to back then. I sat across from the priest and decided I would initiate the conversation. "If it's okay with you Father, I'm gonna need some alone time today. There are some people I need to visit."

"Absolutely okay John, I have a sermon to fine-tune for tomorrow. Why don't we catch up with each other… Let's say late afternoon?"

"Perfect, Father," I reply as a huge serving of eggs and bacon arrive in front of me. "I could easily get used to this every day, thank you Mildred…looks delicious."

"Want to read the paper, John?" He offers the newspaper across the table. "Kennedy was campaigning at the University of Michigan yesterday talking about something called a Peace Corps, which he wants to establish if he's elected. I tell you, having the first Catholic president would really be good for the Church, both in our country and around the world. It's an exciting prospect and I actually think he can win. He dominated Nixon in that debate on Thursday night! Did you catch any of that?"

I thought for a moment before crafting my response. "Yeah, it wasn't even close...He had Nixon sweating bullets. (*I actually wasn't lying, I did watch it but it was many Thursdays ago*). I share your feeling Father, he's very likeable. If I was a gambling man, I'd even bet on him," I answer with my tongue planted firmly in my cheek.

The priest pushes his chair out and as he rises, asks me if I need a ride anywhere since he has some errands to run. I thank him and tell him it looks like a beautiful Indian summer morning (the PC police have yet to be established so I can say 'Indian') to take a long walk after breakfast. He then says goodbye to Mildred and is quickly out the back door to the driveway.

I glance briefly at the sports section. Attention is now shifted from the Yankees' bitter World Series loss, to the NFL for the upcoming Giants vs. Redskins game at Yankee Stadium tomorrow. The article points out the Giants are 3-0 and are favored to win.

I thank Mildred and compliment her cooking, and return to my bedroom to get my hoodie in case it gets cooler later in the day. Autumn weather can change in a split second, even in 1960. I glance again at the clock radio – it's ten minutes past eight. I am out the front door, not having a clue as to what I will do next.

I turn right at the sidewalk and it's a short walk to the corner. I stop and lean against a huge tree that I remember well. Drivers in their cars wait for the turn of the traffic light, each of them about to begin just another day in their ordinary lives. I start to feel misplaced and uneasy. Anxiety begins its hold on me. I realize I am truly not prepared for any of what might occur, but one thing is crystal clear. There appears to be no way out of here...at least for the time being. Lyrics from Bob Dylan's *All Along the Watchtower* enter my subconscious: *"There must be some way out of here, said the joker to the thief, There's too much confusion, I can't get no relief."*

CHAPTER 6

An Encounter with an Old Friend

An older man walks past the rectory and slowly approaches me. As he draws closer he is actually recognizable to me. A white-haired crew cut, heavy frame, and twinkling blue Irish eyes all make it easy for me to recognize Mr. Kelly. Back in the day he would sit on his front porch and greet passersby with an affable "Hello, how are ya doin'?" A cold quart bottle of Ballentine beer was always by his side from which he drew continuous refills. A friendlier old man one could not find anywhere.

And now he approaches me with a "top o' the mornin' – beautiful day, isn't it?"

I react without thinking, "It sure is Mr. Kelly!" *Damn! It's too late now… can't get a do-over on that one!*

"Do I know you sir? If we've met I apologize, I can't remember names very well anymore." He offers his hand in greeting.

As we shake hands I answer "John's the name and I lived on Brooklyn Avenue years ago and right now I'm here on a visit. We didn't know each other very well but I used to pass by your house many times and I remember how kind you were to everyone, especially kids." He stares at me as one does when searching his memory bank to place a name with a face.

Then he smiles and I immediately notice his remaining teeth, stained yellow from a lifetime of cigarettes, probably Pall Mall because I recall they were always longer than regular cigarettes. "It doesn't cost anything to be nice to people, John, I learned that a long time ago…Learned it the hard way. Where you headed? I'm going to the junction, gettin' short on beer and ale. Wanna walk with me?"

I instinctively follow by his side as we cross the intersection realizing I never actually had a real adult-to-adult conversation with Mr. Kelly, no more than a passing hello and maybe tell him where I was going at the time. I have always enjoyed conversations with people older than myself. I come away a little smarter and feeling a lot better, especially if they were reminiscing about a special memory from years ago. So off we go for a little 'grocery shopping'.

He walks slowly, taking small steps. I am guessing he's around seventy-five years old. I wonder about the life experiences he has had. I really know little about him, but I am about to discover the opposite is not true.

"So tell me John, how are your brothers Dominick and Stephen?" He asks without so much as a glance at me as we continue walking.

I am stunned to say the least. *How in God's Name can he know who I am? This is just too bizarre!* I try to collect my thoughts but all I can manage is to answer his question with two of my own questions. "Mr. Kelly, how do you know who I am? Do you really recognize me?"

I must have sounded terrified, as if I was a spy and my cover was blown. "Of course I remember you AND your brothers. You lads were always respectful and polite, every time you walked by my house. I looked forward to seeing you. It was a true bright spot in my day." Now I was really confused. If this is 1960 (and I know it is) the 'John' he knew should be thirteen years old. And why is he talking as if it was years ago when it's not. "You sound surprised, John. I thought we were pretty good friends back then."

"Back when Mr. Kelly? Where the hell I am I? Please tell me what's going on!" Now I was almost indignant. I then gather myself and realize I am yelling at a nice old man who had no part in any of my 'situation.' And if he actually could shed some light on this, I better lighten up on him. "I'm sorry, I didn't mean to shout at you."

"Quite alright lad, considering what you've been through," he said in a very matter-of-fact way, "You still don't know what's happened to you, do you?"

"Why don't you tell me, Mr. Kelly – what do you know?" I am now calm and eager to find out just how much information the old man can give me.

"Well John, haven't you always wished that you could go back in time, even just for a day, to see a time gone by from a brand new perspective? Haven't you secretly longed for this? In fact, haven't you even been obsessed by this wish?"

Oh my God! He knows everything! It has been something I imagined doing but I always realized it could never really happen. I was speechless and he sensed my surprise. "Well John, isn't this what you've been wanting…Or have I got that all wrong? If you care to join me, we're about to have a grand old time together!"

I hear music from a car radio as I am jarred back to a conscious state. Somehow I am still standing against that big tree, alone again. *Was the Mr. Kelly episode just a daydream? He is nowhere to be seen!* The Drifters' *Save the Last Dance for Me* resounds from the open windows of a Mercury Monterrey less than ten feet away. The teenage driver takes a drag from a cigarette and exhales out the window, then leaves rubber as the light turns green.

It all seemed so real…the scene with Mr. Kelly. I backtrack to the rectory, walk onto the driveway where there is a small patio adjacent to the back door. There are a few chairs and a patio table. The chairs are metal and painted a salmon color – the seat back is pressed into a seashell design. I remember they were popular – my grandparents had them on their front porch. I sit down and I can faintly hear Mildred doing the final kitchen cleanup.

I am in isolation and I finally admit something to myself. *I don't want to be here. The Mr. Kelly 'encounter' awakened me. You can never really go back and expect it to be as it was. I am not that kid anymore and I no longer fit in as I had when I was thirteen. But what is my next move? I have only one choice – I trust Father McDonald AND he has offered to help!*

I'll level with him…no more half-truths. I'll make him believe this, and he will figure out a solution for me. I decide to sit here and wait for his return. *That sermon you're working on Father…I might be able to provide you with a whole new angle for it.*

CHAPTER 7
"Kind of Blue"

A crisp autumn breeze creates a swirl of maple leaves drawing my attention. The golden leaves chase each other in a circular motion suspended above the ground, totally controlled by the current and force of the wind.

I am also controlled by some force in this new universe I am now a part of. Unlike the leaf, I can make a decision but I seem to have no control of the outcome. I am subject to the will of a powerful force, one that has granted me a wish based on fantasy which has now become my own bitter reality.

I recall all the *Twilight Zone* episodes I have watched where a helpless character is thrust into a different world, another dimension, and his dilemma consumes him, sometimes driving him to madness. The human brain, though complex and capable of brilliance, can be fragile and vulnerable when its ability to exercise control has been compromised. I am approaching that state of mind but I am not without help. The priest will provide a solution. I simply must believe that.

A man wearing a white sweatshirt and workpants appears from the side of the garage and approaches me. He is an African-American, fairly uncommon to see in this all-white neighborhood in 1960. He greets me and asks if I need any help in finding someone. I suppose it appears odd that a stranger is sitting in the patio of the rectory. As he draws closer I am amazed that I recognize him.

"My name's Robert" as he extends his hand to me. "I am the maintenance man for St Vincent's."

It is indeed Robert, the janitor who was the go-to guy whether it was in the school or the church. He was Johnny-on-the-spot for any task.

"Hi Robert, I'm John. I'm a houseguest of Father McDonald. I'm just waiting for him to return. Nice to meet you."

All the kids knew Robert years ago. He was a friendly guy who always had a smile on his face and a pleasant demeanor. He took his job seriously and seemed grateful to have it. He shoveled snow (no snow blower) in the winter and manicured the lawn, shrubs and bushes in summer. He worked inside the church while we were in class and then cleaned our classrooms and bathrooms after we left the building at three o'clock. He was of a generation that took pride in their work and he did it with a spring in his step and a song in his heart. Back in the day, whenever you saw Robert he was always working.

"You a friend or relative of Father Mac? No matter, a friend of his is a friend o' mine. How long you stayin'?" *Now that, Robert, is a very good question…one that I wish I had an answer for.*

"Just a few days, don't want to overstay my welcome. I'm being treated like a king around here."

Robert flashed a big smile. "Yeah, it's a good place to work - treat me just like family! Say John, can you give me a hand movin' somethin' in the garage? I'm reorganizin' my workshop and this box of wrenches, I'll throw my back out if I move it myself."

"Sure, whatever you need," I answer and follow him as he lifts the garage door revealing spaces for several cars, and a workshop section in the far corner that is 'as neat as a pin'. Garden tools and snow shovels hang from a rack of hooks along the back wall and a huge built-in workbench with a vice attached finish off the space. Then I notice an old wooden rocker next to a shelf with an old record player. "This is a really cool layout you have here Robert," I remark with sincerity and a hint of surprise in my voice. When I was a kid I had no idea of how much this man was responsible for and seeing his 'office' now, makes me appreciate the scope of his job functions. *Whatever he was being paid, it was probably too little...*I thought to myself.

"Yeah, it's like home to me, John." We each grab a handle of a four foot box that weighs a ton and Robert directs me where he wants it located under the workbench out of the way. "Whew! I couldn't have done that myself. I appreciate the help!" He then changes the subject. "You like jazz, John?"

In the last twenty years I have come to like the jazz genre since my daughter Kristin is a jazz pianist and singer. "I do Robert, why do you ask?"

"Well I'm just about to take a break and I always play my jazz records to help me relax. I got some Miles Davis if you don't mind," he said, almost in the form of a question.

"You got the "Kind of Blue' album?" I ask, knowing he would have to have that one. Then I catch myself, not realizing exactly what year this landmark album was actually released.

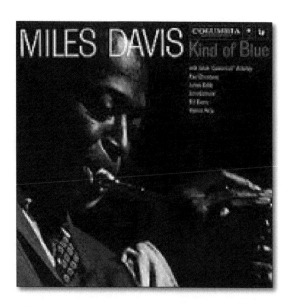

I breathe a sigh of relief when Robert answers "Yeah, I do have it, came out last year. You know your jazz if you on top of that one!" He sounds surprised that a white male in his sixties in 1960 would even know any of this. *And he would be right. Adults in the 50s and 60s were more into 'big band' jazz featuring white musicians*

and singers like Woody Herman and Frank Sinatra, which was much more mainstream. Black artists like Davis and John Coltrane were largely embraced by a black audience who had identified with the complex improvisations that characterized their music.

He carefully lays the record on the turntable and invites me to sit in the rocking chair while he sits on a stool by the workbench. Then it's his turn to surprise me when he says "You a different kinda cat, John. Where you from?"

"I'm from Wisconsin, Robert, but I've lived in a lot of different parts of the country. I was actually born right here in Brooklyn," I respond honestly.

"Somethin' about you that's familiar but I can't rightly say what it is. I'm usually pretty good at readin' people and I don't know why, but I think you probably got somethin' on yo mind that needs tellin'…feel like talkin' 'bout it?"

This guy is a psychic!. He's definitely tuned into my angst after only a few brief minutes. Am I that obvious? "Well, that's why I'm here. Father Mac is helping me deal with some personal problems."

"Yeah he can help ya, he's the best priest in this Church! He's helped me many times when I needed advice. But I found out one thing in my life…Be careful what you want 'cause you might not like it if you get it! Ever have that happen to you?" There is now a brief silence as the album changes tracks.

"Right on man…I mean you're right!" I correct myself quickly since that expression I believe became fashionable later that decade. He looks at me curiously.

"Man, nobody from here talks that jive. Sure you didn't grow up with black folks? You a strange cat, but I mean 'good' when I say that," he quickly adds, assuring me it's a compliment.

I suddenly feel toward Robert as if he is an old friend, someone you could tell a secret to and confide in. There is definitely a kinship growing and I desperately need to let down my guard. I'm thinking Robert is the perfect choice.

"You got some time to talk now?" I ask as we make eye contact.

"Yeah, I'm not on the clock today...Just here to do some personal things. I got all the time you need, man. What's your story, brother?"

CHAPTER 8

THE WHOLE TRUTH AND NOTHING BUT THE TRUTH

I am sitting in the wooden rocker, left leg resting on my right knee, my hands gripping the arms of the chair. *How do I even begin to tell this tale and have any hope that it will be the least bit credible.*

"Robert, I'm going to tell you some things that will be hard to believe but please bear with me. Everything I tell you will be the truth." The man reaches across to the workbench to pick up a pack of Winston's, takes one out and lights up. He takes a drag, exhales, and looks me square in the eyes.

"Go ahead man, I'm all ears. Ain't nothin' gonna shock Robert...I seen and heard it all"

"It all started yesterday." I began. "I actually live in the year 2012, in Wisconsin, but somehow I have been transported back here to 1960, where I grew up as a kid. Since I've been back I have seen and met people I knew back then...including **YOU** Robert!**"

He stared at me, his brow slightly wrinkled as if his brain was trying desperately to process this. Then he took another drag from his cigarette.

I continued. "I know how this must sound but I can prove it to you. As an example, I can promise you that Kennedy will win the election next month. It will be close and it won't be confirmed until the next day but he **WILL** win. I know this because I lived through it when I was thirteen and living on this very street we are on now. We can walk down the block and I can show you the exact house, the address is 1647. I have no idea how any of this happened. I only know I'm here now and I don't know how I can return. That's what's eating me up inside. Robert, you are the first person I've told. Not even Father McDonald knows what I just told you. I was waiting here for him because I was gonna come clean with him too, hoping he had some divine method of getting me back home to 2012. But talking to you, I just felt I could tell you this and you wouldn't think I was crazy. You don't think I'm crazy, do you?"

He strokes his chin with the fingers of his left hand, looks at me and says: "I believe anything can happen. I seen too much to say it can't be true. The Lord can make miracles…Hell, He **has** made miracles so who's to say He can't do this, move you back in time, I mean. What else you remember that's gonna happen? We goin' to war with Russia? What's in store for Kennedy when he's President?"

Oh my God! It only now occurs to me, the horrific events in Dallas on November 22, 1963 that will unfold, as I listen to Robert's barrage of questions! What do I say? How do I answer him?

"Robert, let me say that it will be a challenging presidency, but we will not go to war with Russia." *I think I have dodged the question and try to change the subject.* "You **DO** believe me then?"

"Yeah, I believe you but lemme ask you, if you know what's gonna happen tell me somethin' that's gonna happen soon."

I thought for a moment. "Are you a baseball fan, Robert?"

"Yeah, but not so much since the Dodgers left."

"Well I can tell you that next year, 1961, Roger Maris of the Yankees will hit 61 home runs to break Babe Ruth's record." That's a fact…or **WILL** be a fact, I should say."

"That so? Then maybe I should find me a bookie and make me a wager on that. Or ya think I can get me a bet down like that in Las Vegas?"

"Maybe you can, Robert," I said, slightly regretting that I was encouraging him to make a bet with *insider* information. "Anyway Robert, what would you do if you were me in this situation?"

"Man this is way beyond me – ya gotta see Father Mac on this stuff. I just keep this church buildin' running. I got no line to the top like he does. What else can you tell me about what's comin' up?"

Side one of *Kind of Blue* finishes and he shuts off the record player. "John, I told ya about wantin' somethin' so much, and then gettin' it ain't all it's cracked up to be. This here thing that's happened to you, just what I'm sayin'."

I lean back in the rocker, realizing I have unburdened myself, but without any resolution coming from it. As Robert places the record back into its jacket, I close my eyes to rest them for a few moments. I don't know how long I may have dozed off to sleep. When I awaken, Robert is gone. There is a middle-aged man leaning under the hood of a car in the garage with his back to me. He removes the dipstick to check the oil level, wipes it clean and then replaces it back in the engine. He hasn't yet noticed me sitting here. Finally he turns around to reach for a can of oil on the shelf. I am stunned when I see his face. I grasp the arms of the rocker, goose bumps washing over my entire body. I am visibly shaken, initially recoiling backward and then leaning forward to be certain my eyes are not deceiving me. They are not. The man flashes a brilliant smile as he acknowledges my presence. This man is my father!

CHAPTER 9

RESOLUTION

It seems longer, but for only a few seconds my eyes are fixated on my father's face. It is a face far different than the last time I saw him alive. That was three years ago on his 90th birthday when it was obvious that advanced age had drawn deep lines in his face. He had a faraway look in his eyes, and dementia had robbed him of coherency and concentration. I am now looking at a vibrant, energetic man of only forty-one years old, twenty-three years my junior.

"It's about time we got together, John. How are you, son? You look good!" We approach each other and embrace. I hug him tightly, not wanting to let go fearing he would vanish if I loosen my grip. I am still not believing I am in his presence. I back off, but both my hands continue holding onto his face, ensuring this is no apparition. I am welling up with uncontrollable emotion and tears begin to form and run down my cheek. I quickly wipe them dry with my sleeve. "It's okay John, I know this is difficult for you," he says reassuringly.

"Dad, what am I doing here in 1960? Do you know how or why any of this is happening to me?" *I am now begging for clarity and some sense of purpose and I have a feeling my father can help me understand.*

He grabs a shop rag and wipes his hands, then extends his right arm over my left shoulder. "John, why don't we go inside and talk about this," and he points to the rectory.

"You have permission to go inside…Since when Dad?"

"Let's just say I have special clearance for today," he smiles and I follow him through the back door. We pass through the kitchen, nodding and smiling at Mildred, and proceed to the living room. As I enter I am stunned and taken aback by what I see.

Fathers Murphy and Spengler are seated on the sofa, Robert is standing in front of the fireplace, and Mr. Kelly is sitting in an easy chair sipping on a cold mug of beer. In the center of the room stands Father McDonald. All eyes are now on me.

"What is this, Father McDonald, some sort of intervention?" I ask with a bit of a New York attitude in my tone.

"You could call it that John. We need to talk. Would you like something to drink? Mildred has Pepsi, iced tea, or milk in the refrigerator."

"I'll have what Mr. Kelly's having." Father Murphy chuckles as Robert goes into the kitchen, returning with a cold bottle of Miller High Life. Mr. Kelly lets loose with a combination of a laugh and his patented twenty second coughing spasm. I remember it well.

"This should make you feel at home John," Robert says in an obvious reference to Milwaukee's hometown brew.

Father Mac continues. "The last two days have been challenging for you, have they not, he asked rhetorically.

But the truth is, you have been wishing and hoping to come back here for a very long time. Isn't that true?"

I do not answer. *I suddenly feel as if I am on trial.*

"John, you have spent many years applauding life as it was in the middle of the 20th century. Some might say you characterize it as idyllic! But John, the 1960s in particular, were a far cry from *Nirvana*, if I can borrow a metaphor from our Hindu brethren. If you recall, it was a decade of three horrible assassinations, racial unrest and bigotry, a most unpopular war in Vietnam, and the threat of Communism lurking in our midst. Have you forgotten how tough it was for our country to get through all that?"

My father picked it up here. "John, what Father Mac is really saying is that you can never go back to a time where you no longer belong and expect it to be as it was. You're no longer a kid. No one wants to take away your fond memories but each of us has to learn to move forward and be comfortable with any changes that occur throughout our lifetimes. God blessed me with a long life. I lived nine decades and each one was a challenge. I had to learn to adjust to many changes and it wasn't always easy. Hanging on too tightly to the past, well let's just say...It's not always a good thing."

I sit stone-faced, glaring at each of them, feeling almost betrayed. I feel like the last person to discover a secret, or the victim of a schoolyard prank. *It was all a well-conceived plot and they were all complicit.*

Father Spengler then pipes in. "John no one's saying you can't be proud of your past, where you came from, and all you've accomplished. But give the next generation a break. We're all in this together. Let them make their own mark. Try not to be too *preachy*, if I can use that word," he said forcing a slight smile. "Can you give that some thought when you go back?"

I looked at Father Mac. "Father, why did you string me along for the last two days when you were fully aware of my situation?"

"I had to gain your trust, John…We all did. And you needed to figure it out by yourself. Now you've done that and our work is finished."

"So what happens now?" I looked at Father Mac.

"Robert will handle the details of your re-entry back to 2012," the priest responded.

My father approaches me with a look of compassion and assurance. "John, please don't worry, we will see each other again. And you'll see mother and all the people you missed the most. I promise you that." We embrace and a feeling of peacefulness envelops me, as if a huge burden is finally lifted from me.

Robert motions me to follow him and we head toward his workshop. "Have a seat in the rocker, John, and rest your eyes," he directs. He turns on the record player and the smooth sound of Miles Davis' trumpet sends me into a deep sleep.

Time passes and my eyes open. I see a cocktail glass filled with ice – the contents are a gold hue in color. I raise the glass and sniff. The aroma is unmistakably Scotch Whiskey, Johnny Walker Black on the rocks with a splash of water, my drink of choice for years.

I hear a woman's voice singing a familiar song...

Since you went away, the days grow long,
And soon I'll hear ol' winter's song.
But I miss you most of all my darling,
When autumn leaves start to fall

It is *Autumn Leaves,* one of my favorite jazz standards and the voice is more than recognizable. I look up onto a stage and see my daughter Kristin singing and playing the piano! In the center of the table is a promotional tent card reading: **Welcome to the "Artists' Quarter," the premier jazz club in St. Paul. Tonight featuring The Kristin Sponcia Quartet!** I am blown away! Seated across from me is my daughter-in law Paj. To my left is my son Jeff and on my right is my wife Joyce. Their eyes are riveted on Kristin, feeling a sense of pride and enjoyment in her celebrity.

It's as if I had never left. I feel as if no one even knew I was gone. It would be naïve of me to tell anyone of my experiences over the past two days. It's not the least bit credible to anyone but me. I pick up my glass and take a long sip. I set the glass down on the coaster and watch the condensation descend from the cold glass. I take a deep breath and exhale in complete relaxation. There is a certain peacefulness that washes over me. I am now totally comfortable with who I am, where I am, and my place in time. *I can now move forward after going back.* I know I needed to make that journey back…But I also know I won't need to do it again.

Made in the USA
Middletown, DE
08 December 2022

17636379R10043